Pearl,

Hope you enjoy the adventures on the Great Lakes!

Let the adventures begin!

Tyler S Benson

D1032868

The Adventures of Onyx
and
The Guardians
of the Straits

by Tyler Benson

Ensign Benson Books LLC

Illustrations by David Geister
Design by Joe Fahey

Ensign Benson Books LLC
1323 Kieran Court
Petoskey, MI 49781
www.adventuresofonyx.com
ensignbensonbooks@gmail.com

Printed and bound in the United States of America

Second Edition

10 9 8 7 6

LCCN 2012906563

ISBN 978-0-615-62737-3

This book was expertly produced by Book Bridge Press.
www.bookbridgepress.com

book bridge press sm

Dedicated to my daughters, Olivia Jean, Annie Elizabeth, and Charlotte Marie, and to all Coastie Kids.

I hope this story, and the many stories to come, will help you feel a little closer to your dad or mom when they are away serving and protecting this great nation. And I hope that these Adventures of Onyx will teach you the same core values that the Coast Guard teaches us: Honor, Respect, and Devotion to Duty.

One rainy evening, a homeless dog, lost and without a purpose, wandered onto the grounds of a Coast Guard Station in St. Ignace, Michigan. She was looking for shelter from the cold rain. She walked to the docks where a Coast Guard boat was tied up and found an open hatch. The wet dog climbed aboard the boat and settled comfortably into the rescue compartment.

Suddenly an alarm sounded. The hair on the dog's neck raised up, and she looked around for the source of the sound. Four people quickly came aboard. They were members of the United States Coast Guard.

Dean, the lead Coastie, told the other crewmembers about a freighter that was in trouble.

"An 800-foot freighter passing through the Straits of Mackinac has two injured crewmembers aboard," Dean said. "A medical evacuation has been requested. Take your positions!"

The other Coasties agreed with a united "Aye, aye!"

The boat launched into action, the siren sounded, and the Coast Guard motor lifeboat headed into Lake Huron with the dog still onboard.

Soon after, Hogan went into the compartment where the dog was hiding to get the emergency medical kit prepared. Seeing the man, the frightened dog backed further under the seat.

As Hogan prepared the kit, an oxygen tank slipped from his hands and rolled next to the dog's paw. Hogan saw the dog and jumped back in surprise.

"Where did you come from?" he asked.

Just then, Evans entered the compartment and found Hogan with the dog.

"Hogan!" Evans said. "What is that dog doing onboard?"

"I don't know," Hogan said. "I found her hiding in here when I came to get our rescue equipment."

"Well, secure that dog," Evans said. "And get ready. The freighter is closer than we thought. It's just off of the Mackinac Bridge, and we have an estimated arrival time of 10 minutes."

Hogan petted the nervous dog and told her, "You stay here, girl. I'll be right back."

Up on deck, Pelkey spotted the freighter.

"There it is!" she shouted. "Starboard side!"

As the Coast Guard boat came alongside the freighter, Pelkey got on the radio.

"Motor Vessel Pride of the Lakes, Motor Vessel Pride of the Lakes," Pelkey called to the freighter. "This is the United States Coast Guard. Prepare your injured crewmen for transfer."

Dean yelled over the wind and rain to Evans and Hogan on the bow, "Here we go, gentlemen. By the book!"

The men aboard the freighter frantically prepared for the transfer. They slipped and slid on the deck as they strapped their injured shipmates into stretchers. Then they carefully lowered the first injured man from the freighter deck to the Coasties waiting on the rescue boat below. Despite the wind and rain, the first transfer went smoothly.

As the second injured crewman was being transferred, the boat was slammed by a powerful wave. The Coast Guard boat and the freighter crashed against each other violently. Just then, lightning flashed and thunder boomed! The startled men on the freighter accidentally dropped the stretcher, and the second injured man fell helplessly into the sea.

"Man overboard!" Hogan yelled.

"Prepare for a recovery!" Dean yelled back.

Pelkey ran down to the main deck to prepare for a waterside pickup.

Hogan and Evans quickly took the first injured crewman down below where he would be safer.

"You stay here," Hogan said.

"What about my shipmate?" the injured crewman yelled.

"Don't worry, Sir," Evans said. "We'll save him." Hogan and Evans quickly ran back outside.

Inside the compartment the dog watched. She heard the man yell, "Oh no! He is strapped in and face down!"

The man suddenly saw the dog and made eye contact with her. Tears began to roll down the scared, worried, and injured crewmember's face. He wanted to help, but he was helpless.

"My shipmate is in trouble," he said to the dog. "My friend is in trouble."

The dog watched it all. She saw the fear. She heard the screams. Suddenly, something inside her ignited. It burned like a fire. A sensation she had never felt before washed over her. She felt a sense of greater purpose, a sense of servitude, a sense of something important and larger than herself. She knew what she needed to do. She was no longer a lost dog. She was a dog with a newfound purpose.

The dog sprinted for the ladder.

As the Coast Guard boat was approaching the injured man in the water, the dog saw the overturned stretcher.

Seeing the dog on deck, Hogan yelled, "What are you doing out here, girl? Get back down below where it is safe!"

Just then the dog let out a loud, confident bark and selflessly leapt into the heavy seas.

With all of her might she swam for the man. She swam as hard as she could. She swam until it burned in her muscles. She swam through the howling wind and the cold sea. Fear didn't stand in her way. A newfound bravery pushed her through. The Coasties watched the dog swim on, only so another may live.

The dog finally made it to the man in the heavy seas. The waves dunked the man's head up and down. He looked over and saw the dog.

Cold and in shock, he yelled to her, "Help me, dog! Please help me!"

The dog put her paws up on the capsized stretcher and swam with all her might. She pushed and pushed and pushed until a miracle happened! The dog righted the stretcher, saving the man from trouble.

The dog stayed with the man as the Coast Guard boat came alongside. The Coasties quickly reached overboard and pulled the man and the dog onboard.

The exhausted dog couldn't even stand up.

Pelkey and Evans quickly took the injured man down below, where his relieved shipmate was waiting.

Hogan wrapped the dog in a blanket, picked her up in his arms, and headed to the back deck of the boat. He dropped to his knees and looked at the miracle dog that he held in his arms.

"Ha ha!" Dean yelled from the driver's chair. "I don't know where that dog came from, but thank goodness for her!"

Hogan looked up at Dean. "Onyx," he told him. "Her name is Onyx. She is a Guardian like one of us!"

"I believe it!" Dean said.

The Coast Guard boat headed for the station.

Back on deck, Pelkey dropped to her knees and started petting the wet dog. "The station has been looking for a good morale dog, and this hero may be just what we're looking for."

Hogan stood up and Onyx stood beside him. The rain was letting up, the seas were laying down. Hogan put a small orange life jacket on Onyx and adjusted the straps. Then he cut the excess strap off and put it around her neck, making a collar.

"There," he said. "Perfect. Now you look like a true Coast Guard Morale Dog."

Pelkey smiled and nodded her head, agreeing as she headed up the ladder to the bridge to take her seat next to Dean.

Dean nodded to Pelkey and said, "Onyx, huh? I like that!"

Dean looked forward. The storm had passed and the rising morning sun was breaking through the clouds. Fair winds and following seas had come to the morning Straits of Mackinac.

"All right, you guys!" he yelled out. "Secure the deck. We're heading for home. Coming up!"

Dean put the throttles down and steered the Coast Guard boat for home, into the sunrise. It is a new day. It is a new beginning. For today begins . . .

The Adventures of Onyx and the Guardians of the Straits.

GREAT LAKES AUTHOR **Tyler Benson** is from St. Louis, Michigan. He has served in the United States Coast Guard for more than a decade in St. Ignace, Michigan. He began writing short stories about his search and rescue adventures in the Coast Guard to educate his three young daughters about what Daddy does when he goes on duty for 48 hours at a time. He wanted his daughters to learn the importance of service to their country and helping those in need. To help his daughters better understand his job, Tyler wrote the stories featuring his real station's morale dog, Onyx. These stories soon evolved into a dream. This dream would be a tribute and a way to bring recognition to all who serve or have served in the United States Coast Guard. Tyler welcomes all to join his family, friends, station, shipmates, and Onyx as they get underway. A storm is on the horizon, a hero will rise—let the adventures begin!